Weather

George Ivanoff

Weather can be hot.

Weather can be wet.

I like hot weather!
I like the sun.

I put on a hat.
I put on sunscreen.

I like cold weather!
I like the snow.

I put on a warm hat.
I put on gloves.

I like wet weather!
I like the rain.

I put on a raincoat.
I put on boots.
I hide when it rains.

I like windy weather!
I like to see the leaves move.

I put on a warm top.
It is hard to fly in the wind.

I like stormy weather!
I like the lightning.

I put on my slippers.
I stay inside.
I hide when I hear thunder.

Weather changes all the time.
What is the weather like today?

Match these things to the weather.

Hot weather

Cold weather

Wet weather

Windy weather

Stormy weather

I like hot weather!
I like the sun.

Weather can be wet.

Curly and Ladybird pulled and pulled.
"We can't pull the berry down," said Curly.